PEGASUS RISING
AND OTHER STORIES

Collins

Contents

Unit 8

Core: Fantastic Monsters 6

Challenge: Pegasus Rising 22

Unit 9

Core: Roman Life 38

Challenge: The Goddess of Discord 54

Fantastic Monsters

Written by Liz Miles

Illustrated by Vlad Stankovic

Films, books and video games are full of fairies, dragons and powerful beasts. People all around our planet have enjoyed the legends that surround these fantastical creatures for thousands of years. But where did these stories come from?

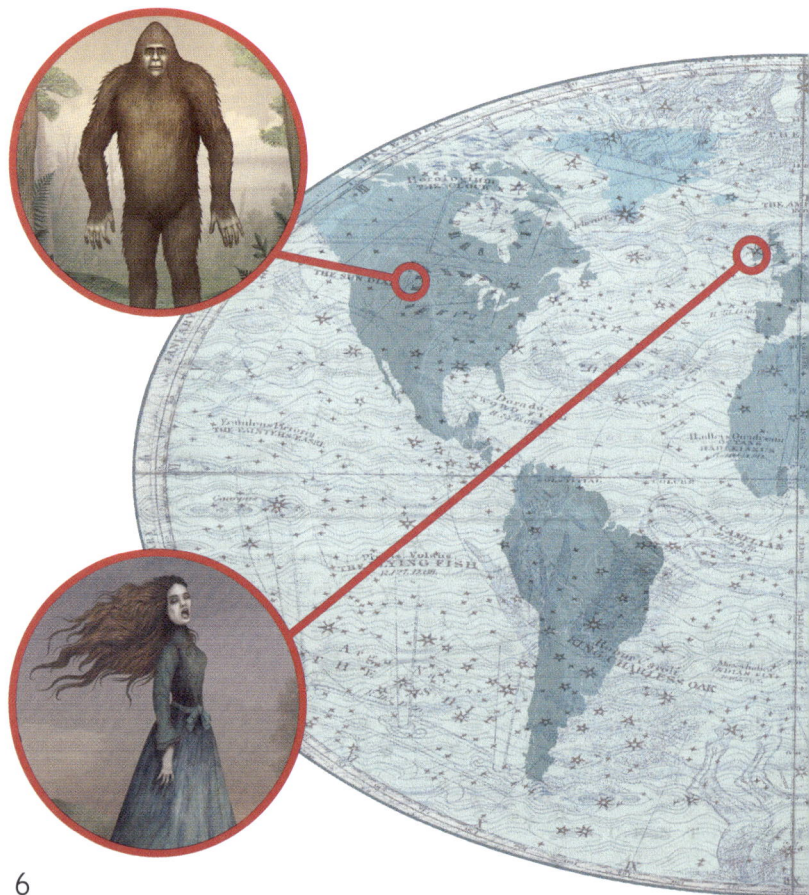

People who study different cultures are interested in stories about fantastical creatures. That's because these stories give clues about what people from different cultures believe. It turns out that there are many similarities between stories about spirits and monsters across history, places and cultures.

Let's look at the origins of some of these creatures.

The sound of bad luck

Meet the **banshee**, a female spirit from Irish-Celtic folktales. Her name means 'woman of the fairy mound'. She is described as having ragged hair, a torn gown and a spine-chilling wail.

Legends say that the sound of a banshee's screams outside a house predict that someone in that family will die.

The idea of predicting bad luck is common to cultures around the globe. Like banshees, the following creatures are believed to predict doom:

- A hooting owl (South Africa)
- One magpie by itself (UK)
- A black moth in the house (Mexico)
- A black cat crossing your path (Japan)

Minding the wild

Some monsters from legends protect wild places or keep humans from harm.

Bigfoot, or **Sasquatch**, is sacred to the Sts'ailes people of British Columbia. They recount how this giant, hairy, ape-like monster protects their forests and mountains in North America.

Different accounts of this creature describe it as foul-smelling and strong enough to destroy trees. Some say it steals fish and leads people astray until they get lost.

If you found out about a beast like this roaming in a forest, would you want to find it or keep well away? Perhaps people told Sasquatch's story to keep enemies away.

Destroy ... or bring joy?

Dragons are extremely popular in stories and art from all around the globe. There are some interesting differences in accounts of dragons from different places.

Most dragons in Western legends are fire-breathing monsters that kill and destroy. They look like lizards with wings and are often shown with clouds of steam billowing from their noses. Fearless humans slay them to show their bravery.

However, dragons in Eastern legends are not evil, and often bring joy. They do not have wings but slither across the sky like serpents. In China, dragons are loyal creatures. Some people link them with good luck. Some legends say they can make it rain when crops are dry.

Look out around water!

The **bunyip** lives in lagoons, waiting to pounce on unsuspecting victims. The Wemba-Wemba people in Victoria and New South Wales describe it as a powerful water spirit with a rounded skull and sharp fangs. The Wemba-Wemba avoid water when they hear its loud cry. Legend says it devours people.

In Japanese culture, stories of the **kappa** remind people of the dangers of lingering by water, too. This turtle-like monster is said to drown its victims. But a gift of a cucumber or a polite bow might save you.

Because of this legend, Japanese cooks invented a kind of sushi with cucumber, called 'kappa-maki'.

What lurks in the deep?

People have told stories of **mermaids and mermen** for thousands of years. In Greek legends, the sea god, Triton, is a merman. Mermaids often appear in love stories and use their voices to bewitch sailors. Never annoy a mermaid, as some tales say they drown people when they are angry.

In 1493, the explorer Columbus recounted seeing three mermaids. In fact, tales of mermaids and mermen appear in nearly all cultures where people go on sea voyages.

Some of these tales might have come about because humans want to explain the secrets and dangers of the deep sea.

Sea serpents can be found in old stories from crews of terrified sailors. These monster-sized snakes suddenly rise from the deep. Legends blame them for shipwrecks.

Some people believe giant squids inspired stories about sea serpents. Giant squids have long bodies and tentacles that sailors could mistake for snake-like sea creatures.

Do *you* think any of these fantastical creatures exist?

Fantastical creatures around us

If you keep an eye out, you might spot fantastical creatures in all sorts of places.

This Scottish silver coin celebrates the unicorn. The unicorn appears on the Scottish royal coat of arms, too. It represents power and pride.

Dragon lanterns are popular around Chinese New Year. They stand for good luck.

The griffin is common on coats of arms in lots of places. It often represents strength, bravery and leadership.

The Welsh flag has shown a red dragon on a white and green background since 1959. But the red dragon has been an emblem of Wales since 655 CE.

Pegasus Rising

Written by Lindsay Galvin

Illustrated by Kayleigh Efird

Hello. I'm Pegasus. Yes, the amazing Pegasus. That beautiful white horse with giant wings, who ended up as stars in the sky.

The way I entered life was iconic, but ... gross. I was the child of a snake-haired monster who had to be destroyed for me to be born. That's right, I sprang out of the decapitated Medusa.

One minute the demigod Perseus fights her, the next – ouch – there I am. It gave me little respect for demigods.

But when I unfurled my shiny new wings and took off, I felt a burst of joy. I laughed at the brown horses grounded on the mountains below.

I spent most of my time doing what I'm made for: flying. I delighted in my freedom. The sky was my playground, and the clouds were my toys.

Humans did try to capture me, but I never got too grouchy about it. Humans see something wild and want to ride it, tame it, or destroy it. And let's face it, I'm pretty wild!

Some people tried ropes and nets. Some even attempted to use music as a decoy. If the sounds weren't too horrible, I'd allow them to get close. But then I'd flick back my mane, scrape the ground and unfurl my wings. I'd swoop high and leave them choking in the dust, disappointed.

Then came Bellerophon. He strutted up as I was sipping from a mountain spring. I must admit: the boy had swagger.

I frowned when I noticed something coiled around his hand. It was a golden bridle, glowing with the goddess Athena's blessing.

When a goddess decides to meddle, danger is bound to be brewing.

But I found myself bending my neck and allowing the boy to slip the bridle on, and I felt the bit in my mouth.

The next minute, he'd mounted onto my back, shouting, "Look at me! I'm invincible!"

I should have thrown the boy, but I took off. The ground dropped away, his shouts filled the air and ... I didn't totally hate him being with me.

I could see the point of having a rider. The boy allowed me to really show what I could do. We clowned around over villages, enjoying the astounded shouts from below.

But soon the boy went looking for danger. And that's how we were employed to defeat a vile monster.

The beast was part-lion and part-goat, with a snake's tail. It was powerfully ugly. And it breathed fire!

We swooped in and I dodged the flames. Bellerophon peppered the beast with arrows, toying with it and showing off to the crowd.

Finally, Bellerophon hurled a spear into the monster's mouth. The heat melted it, and the monster choked.

Who got all the credit for the monster's defeat? Bellerophon. But he wouldn't have beat it without my flying and dodging.

After that, it was all victory parades and feasts. Royalty praised Bellerophon. Music played, with every tune about the new demigod. Crowds surrounded us as we travelled around the towns. Children pointed at me in amazement – then forgot me when Bellerophon strutted by.

Bellerophon's ego grew. One morning, he announced, "Pegasus, next stop is the home of the gods! I've shown the gods that I'm just as good as they are, so I deserve to meet them."

The boy needed to get his feet back on the ground. But with a flying horse as his mount, that wasn't happening. I told him not to go, but humans never listen.

So, off we went on a voyage beyond the clouds, to the home of the gods. The King of the Gods regarded us. I knew he was annoyed. I expected a thunderbolt at any moment.

"See, Pegasus, the gods love me!" shouted Bellerophon.

But the King of the Gods wasn't going to allow this proud human a noble end.

He sent … a fly.

The fly bit me, so I bucked and threw Bellerophon off my back. He bounced on the ground, wailing loudly.

Bellerophon survived, but he was broken and bitter. Dented pride hurts deeper than broken bones.

The gods decided I was too good for the human planet. They lifted me into the night sky, where I now shine as a pattern of stars. Immortal.

Do I ever miss showing off with that silly boy? Don't tell the gods, but maybe just a little.

Horses in legends and fables

Horses, like Pegasus, feature in many legends and fables.

Unicorn

'Unicorn' means 'one horn', as this horse-like animal is depicted with a single, pointed horn. In some accounts, the unicorn's horn is said to have the power to make poisoned water safe to drink, and to heal sickness.

Hippogriff

'Hippogriff' combines the Greek term 'hippo' (meaning horse) with 'griffin'. This beast is described as being part-horse, part-eagle and part-lion.

Kelpie

Kelpies are horse-like monsters from Scottish legends. They are said to be found lurking near fast rivers or deep lakes, and gallop into the depths of the water to drown any humans that try to ride them.

Hippocampus

The hippocampus is a part-horse, part-fish sea creature from Greek legends. The term 'hippocampus' uses the Greek terms 'hippos' and 'kampos' (meaning sea monster).

Roman Life

Written by Liz Miles

Illustrated by Rudolf Farkas

Is it true that Rome is named after a boy raised by a wild animal?

Yes! Rome is an impressive city that's about 3,000 years old. According to legend, it was founded by twins named Romulus and Remus in 753 BCE. The myth says these twins were orphaned and raised by a wild dog until a shepherd found them. When they grew up, they were ready to build their own town.

But when they couldn't agree on where to put it, Romulus ended up killing Remus and naming Rome after himself!

Rome started as a little settlement in a valley but grew into the centre of the Roman Empire. As the empire spread, people moved there from places as far away as Africa.

Rome was a diverse city with lots of rules. It was home to all kinds of people, from powerful emperors, to those with no rights at all.

Could anyone gain power?

Not everyone could gain power in Rome. The power system meant men ruled, both in public and at home.

Originally, a king ruled Rome. Later it became a republic, which didn't allow a single ruler. Instead, a group of wealthy men, called the Senate, ruled.

a meeting of the Senate

Common people who were male could vote but didn't have much power. Typically, this group included people like farmers or craftsmen who didn't have enough wealth or status to be in the Senate. Enslaved people were below the common class.

As the Roman Empire spread, single rulers returned. This time, instead of a king, Rome had an emperor – the top-ranking male leader.

Men were head of the household.

What about women?

The power system meant women weren't allowed to vote or hold public roles. Most women didn't have their own wealth and had to depend on the male head of the household.

However, it's a myth that women never had any control. Around 2,000 years ago, crowds of women protested in the streets against a rule that restricted their clothing choices. They were told they could no longer dress in certain shades, including purple. Their protest meant the rule was scrapped.

Women often married when they were teenagers. They were expected to focus on their family's needs at home. Many did not go to school. However, some found jobs outside their homes, for example, as midwives and priestesses.

Some women could influence their powerful husbands. A wealthy woman named Plotina spoke up for people's rights. When her husband became emperor, she promised the crowds she would still support them now that she was empress.

bust of Plotina

Didn't everyone live in fancy villas?

Wealthy Romans had pleasant houses in Rome, as well as beautiful villas outside the town that they used as holiday homes. Typically, their living spaces surrounded a large room, called an atrium, with an opening in the roof. Symmetrical pillars, archways and mosaics gave a grand feel.

remains of a villa

Common people lived in blocks of flats spread across Rome. As most Romans lived in crowded spaces, health was important. Gyms and public baths helped keep people healthy – they were popular places to hang out, too.

ruins of a gym

Did they really use communal toilets?

Wealthy Romans had private toilets, below-ground heating systems and private rooms for bathing at home. However, common people had to use public toilets or empty pots into drains. Public toilets were often next to public baths and were less clean than toilets today.

To keep the streets clean and prevent dreadful diseases from spreading, city planners created pipe systems to carry toilet waste away.

underground heating system

Why were public baths so popular?

Romans enjoyed going to public baths to chat and relax. People from all classes visited the baths daily because they believed it kept them healthy.

A typical bathing method was to go from a tepid room to a hot room to sweat, then leap into a cold plunge pool. This was said to cleanse and invigorate their bodies.

Roman bath remains

Romans even chatted while sitting on public toilets!

Were there female gladiators?

Yes! For entertainment, people flocked to arenas like the Colosseum to see chariot races and thrilling, physical games. Colosseum fighters were called gladiators, and included both men and women.

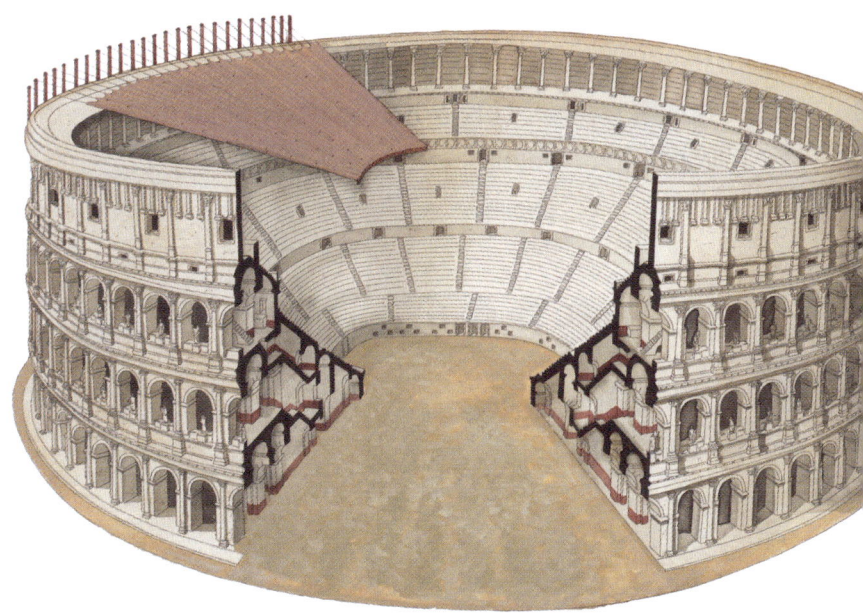

The Colosseum could hold up to 50,000 spectators.

Gladiators achieved wealth and fame, but they faced the threat of death. Some even had to fight wild animals like lions and tigers. They used weapons, including three-pronged tridents, and nets and shields to defend themselves.

Things the Romans left behind

We can see clues about Roman life today, with well-preserved ruins and artefacts.

Gold, copper, silver and brass coins are frequently found and studied by historians.

Mosaics have survived for thousands of years.

You can see the remains of an underground pipe system.

Roman toilets have been found in Turkey, Italy and the UK.

The remains of monuments like the Colosseum are still standing 2,000 years on, even after extreme weather and conflicts.

Well-preserved Roman roads are still used in many places across the former Roman Empire.

The Goddess of Discord

Written by Jonny Walker

Illustrated by Alessandra Vitelli

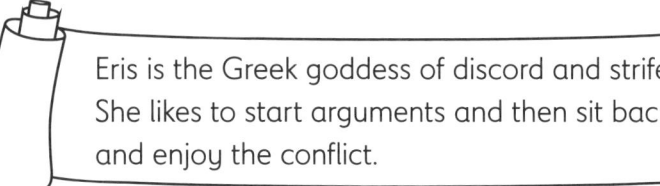

Eris is the Greek goddess of discord and strife. She likes to start arguments and then sit back and enjoy the conflict.

Eris, the Goddess of Discord

The dreadful goddess, Eris,
Devises a cunning plan
To spread some hateful mayhem
Within her mythic clan.

"I'll ruin each Olympian's life,
I'll hassle every god
And each goddess that I detest
Because they say I'm odd.

I have no crown atop my head,
Unlike the Lightning Lord.
But there's method to my badness,
I'm the Goddess of Discord!"

And so, she summons up a mist
And spreads it through the land.
Then every human, god and beast
Wakes up to take a stand.

The dragons growl within their lairs,
The kings wake bathed in sweat.
The gods that tread the mountaintops
Shout, "You ain't seen anythin' yet!"

And Eris smiles an evil grin,
Sits by the River Styx,
And grabs her box of popcorn
To spy on those she tricks.

The Cyclops is the monster-child of the God of the Seas. He distrusts people who invade his space.

Cyclops, the one-eyed giant

The Cyclops, sleeping by the sea,
Dreams up a simple ploy.
He staggers to the clifftop
To threaten a teenage boy.

"Oi, you there! Mortal manchild!
You men, sailing in your ships!
What do you think it sounds like
When a linen sailcloth rips?"

And then the Cyclops hurls a rock
That destroys the weathered sail
And punches a hole in the ship.
The boy cries out and wails!

The boy sinks in the moon-drenched sea,
And begins to gasp for air.
The water takes him to his death –
An ending so unfair.

A man shouts from his sinking ship
And threatens his revenge,
"You killed my boy, you savage beast,
His death will be avenged!"

And down beside the River Styx,
Eris observes with glee,
As raging hatred spreads and grows
Within her enemies.

Athena is the powerful goddess of wisdom, skill and battle-planning. She is famed for her strength and her intellect.

Athena, the Goddess of Wisdom

Athena, mighty goddess,
Lands on Athens' battlefield
As fighters far from Sparta
Start to see their fates revealed.

So many times in her long life,
Under a deathless moon,
Athena's seen a scene like this,
But for them, death comes soon.

The sweating Spartans meet their end,
They scream – that horrid sound!
Athena's owl flits through the blades
That knock them to the ground.

"Wisdom," Athena whispers,
"Is to look upon the dead
With wide and wise unblinking eyes,
Where poppies will bloom red."

She delights in the mystery,
The dance of life and death,
And absorbs the fighters' wisdom
Whispered in their dying breath.

> Scylla is a sea-monster who threatened sailors who came too close. Myrina is a queen of the Amazons, a much-feared team of female fighters.

Scylla, the multi-headed sea monster

"Who needs wisdom?" Eris spits.
"What do *you* know, Athena?
Being smart is not much fun!
I like to act much meaner!"

Eris looks at the crashing waves:
Apocalyptic weather!
As fearless women fighters
Make a pact to fight together.

"Get ready for this beastess,
Scylla, the six-headed fiend!
Hold steady!" Queen Myrina howls,
"I'll blow her to smithereens!"

The red-haired archer sets aflame
A crystal arrow-head,
And aims it at the many-faced
Monstrosity of dread.

The arrows slam into the seal-like
Blubber of the beast.
She slumps into the dark abyss,
Still dreadful, but deceased.

But Eris cackles knowingly,
"What happens next is wild!
The dead beast's dad will resurrect
His cherished little child!"

> Asterion is part-man, part-bull. Asterion was trapped in a maze by King Minos of Crete, his unkind step-dad.

Asterion, the bull-headed beast

The night of conflict Eris planned
Went just as she predicted.
She'd meant to spoil the actors' lives,
Silent and unscripted.

"Yes, how pleasant!" Eris chants
At each destructive scene.
"This might well be the biggest mess
The Greeks have ever seen!"

She twists the mist inside her fist
And hurls it off to Crete.
It blasts Asterion, the boy
With hooves instead of feet.

This step-child of King Minos
Now gets a whole lot stronger.
He smashes through the labyrinth:
A prisoner no longer.

His heavy tread fills each room.
"Oi, King!" he shouts with scorn,
"I'm here to kill the man who
Entrapped me when I was born!"

The bad king cowers, powerless,
Without weapons, just dread.
He feels the heavy bull breath ...
Then the boy bites off his head!

The night of discord ends

Eris, sitting by the Styx,
Reshapes each mythic story,
Twisting tales of torn-up sails
And making all things gory.

She takes the side of dreadful beasts,
Spreads lies about the gods,
Threatens lowly humans,
Winning – against the odds!

Then just as quickly as it came,
The dreadful discord ends.
Eris did not do a thing!
Well ... that's what she pretends.

"I *need* no crown atop my head,
Unlike the Lightning Lord!
There's method to my badness:
I'm the Goddess of Discord!"

Who is Eris?

Eris appears in Greek mythology as someone who is avoided by many gods and goddesses because of her ability to create conflict.

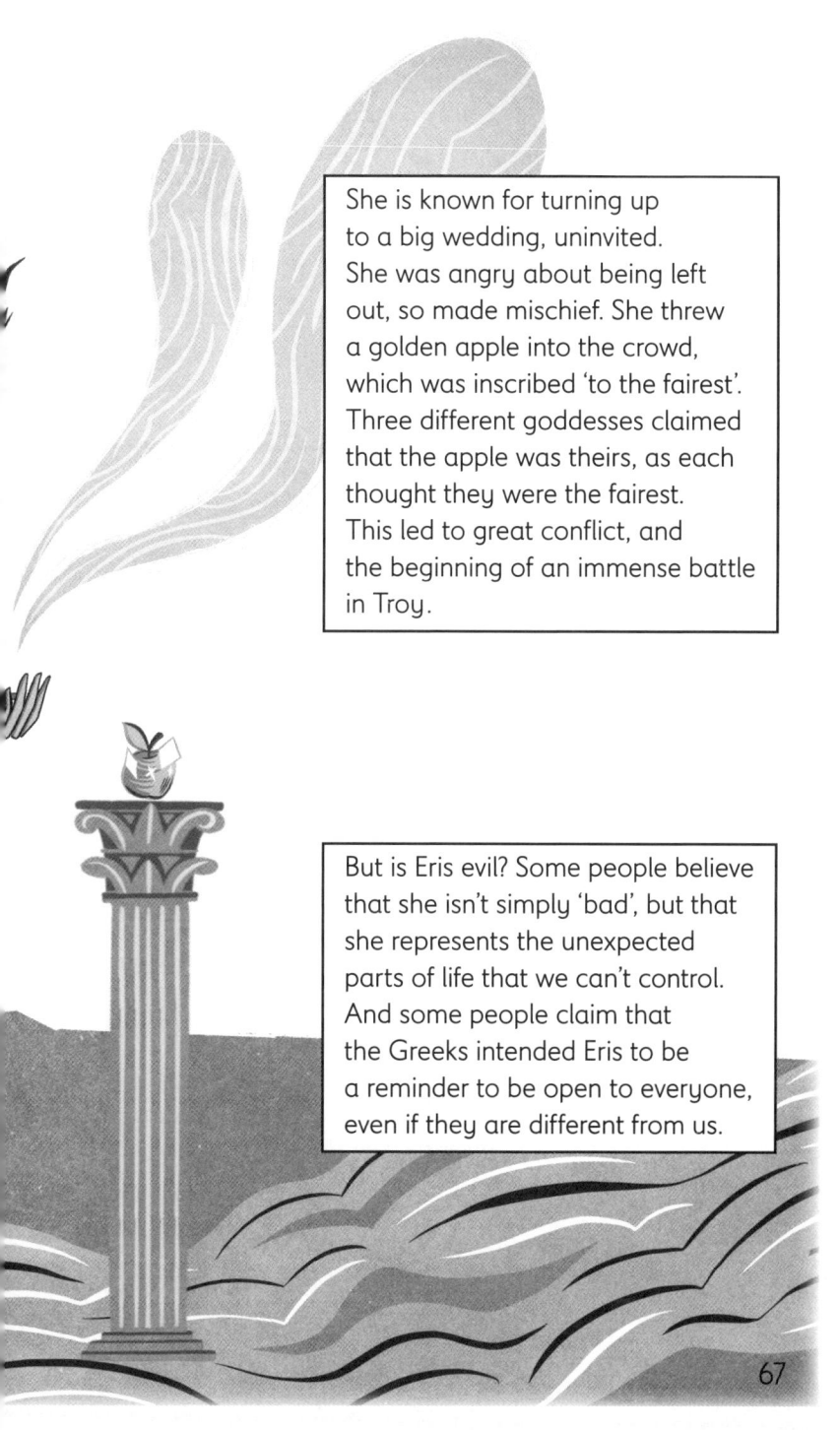

She is known for turning up to a big wedding, uninvited. She was angry about being left out, so made mischief. She threw a golden apple into the crowd, which was inscribed 'to the fairest'. Three different goddesses claimed that the apple was theirs, as each thought they were the fairest. This led to great conflict, and the beginning of an immense battle in Troy.

But is Eris evil? Some people believe that she isn't simply 'bad', but that she represents the unexpected parts of life that we can't control. And some people claim that the Greeks intended Eris to be a reminder to be open to everyone, even if they are different from us.

Acknowledgements

The publishers gratefully acknowledge the permission granted to reproduce the copyright material in this book. Every effort has been made to trace copyright holders and to obtain their permission for the use of copyright material. The publishers will gladly receive any information enabling them to rectify any error or omission at the first opportunity.

p18t Kevin Anderson/Shutterstock, p18b Toa55/Shutterstock, p19t DAWID DOBOSZ/Shutterstock, p19b Tatohra/Shutterstock, pp38–39 Lanmas/Alamy Stock Photo, p40 Lebrecht Music/Alamy Stock Photo, p41 Bridgeman Images, p43 colaimages/Alamy Stock Photo, p44 Dietmar Rauscher/Shutterstock, p45 Stoniko/Shutterstock, p46 dpa picture alliance archive/Alamy Stock Photo, p47l Holmes Garden Photos/Alamy Stock Photo, pp47r & 51t James Caldwell/Alamy Stock Photo, p48 De Agostini/Getty Images, p50tl Sabena Jane Blackbird/Alamy Stock Photo, p50tr Azoor Photo/Alamy Stock Photo, p50b David Stares/Alamy Stock Photo, p51c Dima Moroz/Shutterstock, p51b Robert Estall photo agency/Alamy Stock Photo.

Published by Collins
An imprint of HarperCollins*Publishers*
The News Building, 1 London Bridge Street, London, SE1 9GF, UK

HarperCollins*Publishers*
Macken House, 39/40 Mayor Street Upper, Dublin 1, D01 C9W8, Ireland

Browse the complete Collins catalogue at
collins.co.uk

'Pegasus Rising' text © Lindsay Galvin 2026
All other text, illustrations and design © HarperCollins*Publishers* Limited 2026

Wandle Learning Trust name and logo © Wandle Learning Trust

10 9 8 7 6 5 4 3 2 1

A catalogue record for this publication is available from the British Library.

ISBN 978-0-00-879098-1

All rights reserved. No part of this publication may be reproduced, stored in a retrieval system, or transmitted in any form by any means, electronic, mechanical, photocopying, recording or otherwise, without the prior written permission of the Publisher or a licence permitting restricted copying in the United Kingdom issued by the Copyright Licensing Agency Ltd, 5th Floor, Shackleton House, 4 Battle Bridge Lane, London SE1 2HX.

Without limiting the exclusive rights of any author, contributor or the publisher of this publication, any unauthorised use of this publication to train generative artificial intelligence (AI) technologies is expressly prohibited. HarperCollins also exercise their rights under Article 4(3) of the Digital Single Market Directive 2019/790 and expressly reserve this publication from the text and data mining exception.

Authors: Lindsay Galvin, Liz Miles and
        Jonny Walker
Illustrators: Vlad Stankovic (Advocate Art),
        Kayleigh Efird (Astound US),
        Rudolf Farkas (Beehive Illustration) and
        Alessandra Vitelli (Advocate Art)
Publisher: Katie Sergeant
Product manager: Natasha Paul
Education consultant: Charlotte Raby
Project manager: Emily Hooton
Phonics reviewers: Catherine Baker and
        Abbie Rushton
Proofreader and fact checker: Catherine Dakin
Cover designer: Sarah Finan
Cover illustrator: Kayleigh Efird (Astound US)
Internal designer: 2Hoots Publishing Services Ltd
Production controller: Sophie Waeland

Developed in collaboration with Wandle Learning Trust

Printed in the UK by Martins the Printers

Made with responsibly sourced paper and vegetable ink

Scan to see how we are reducing our environmental impact.

Collins would like to thank Abi Rothe, Nicola Dickens and the schools involved in the Code pilot for contributing to the development of this book.

Access the planning and resources to teach this book at littlewandlecode.org.uk

Going for GOLD

and Other Stories

Collins

Contents

Unit 12

Core: The World of Basketball.............. 6

Challenge: Ouch! 24

Unit 13

Core: Going for Gold 42

Challenge: From Zero To Hero 60

The World of Basketball

Written by Jonny Walker

The world of basketball

The first thing you should know is that I'm not an expert at basketball. But like billions of other people worldwide, I'm *obsessed* with this sport.

Basketball's more than just hurling a ball through a hoop. It's art. It's storytelling. It's life!

The world's top sports by estimated number of fans

Football: 3.5 billion

Cricket: 2.5 billion

Basketball: 2.2 billion

Basketball and me

School life was harsh for a tall, nerdy kid like me. But one day, a basketball coach joined the staff. He was the first person to tell me that being nearly six foot tall at 12 years old could be an advantage.

"Try basketball!" he urged.

So I did. Basketball helped me to work on my self-confidence. Workouts, practice and working with a team became part of my life. I learned about new role models, who opened up a different world to me.

My coach turned basketball into a life lesson about teamwork, consistency, fairness and valuing the 'fundamentals' over 'circus-style' trick shots.

A quote made popular by basketball star Kevin Durant.

This is not a handbook

To confirm, I'm not going to tell you what basketball is, and I'm certainly not going to make you a better player. But what I can do is tell you about the powerful life lessons we can learn from basketball.

Basketball is for everybody ... everywhere.

American children playing in the 1970s.

It's not all about height

It *helps* to be tall if you want to compete at the highest level of basketball. But shortness isn't always a hurdle, and some athletes work to make it an advantage.

At 168 cm, Spud Webb is the third-shortest player in the history of the NBA. He won the Dunk Contest in 1986 and defeated his 203-cm team-mate with two perfect scores!

Modern teams work best when they're made up of players of different sizes, performing different roles.

Being extremely tall can certainly help with rebounding and dunking. The tallest female basketball player was Margo Dydek, who stood at a towering 218 cm!

Average heights in the world

Male   NBA basketball player: 198 cm
         Typical adult: 170 cm

Female WNBA basketball player: 185 cm
         Typical adult: 160 cm

BasketbALL

Everybody should have a chance to play basketball – it's a versatile and adaptable sport. There are contests, teams and clubs worldwide that make basketball inclusive for people of all ages and abilities.

In England, there are over 100 wheelchair basketball clubs. Wheelchair basketball has been a Paralympic sport since 1960. The GB men's team were silver medallists in Paris 2024.

Beyond clubs and teams, many more people just play basketball for fun.

Where I live in London, random games start up whenever people arrive at the park. The sport draws in people of all ages, genders and skill-levels. Between us, we speak English, Arabic, Turkish, Bengali, Lithuanian and Polish, but we communicate through basketball.

Who's the MVP?

Basketball is played in every continent around the world. In the US, it's practically worshipped! The NBA and the WNBA are widely seen as the highest level for basketball players.

Each year, one NBA player is voted as 'MVP', the Most Valuable Player. This means they are considered the best performing player of that season. In recent years, MVPs have come from Canada, Serbia and Cameroon.

2025 MVP, Shai Gilgeous-Alexander

Worldwide appeal

In the UK, football, cricket, rugby, tennis and golf get bigger audiences than basketball … for now! But in Serbia and Lithuania, the sport is thriving – even though they are a world away from the birthplace of basketball in the US.

The love of basketball is spreading across Africa. The first African female player in the WNBA was Mwadi Mabika, born in the Democratic Republic of the Congo. Some top athletes in the men's game are also of African descent. For example, Manute Bol, the tallest player in the world, was from Sudan.

Mwadi Mabika

Manute Bol

Celebrating excellence

Players who have made a significant impact are celebrated in the Basketball Hall of Fame of America. The Hall of Fame also recognises the work of referees, coaches and teams. In 2025, the four-time WNBA champion Sue Bird was judged to be worthy of this accolade.

Hard work pays off – legends are never forgotten. That's why basketball appeals to me. I also love the storytelling of each game, which has all the dramatic twists and turns of a good film or epic myth.

Sue Bird (right)

Who's the GOAT?

Many think LeBron James is the 'GOAT' – Greatest Of All Time.

He first became an NBA player at just 18 years old. In his 40s, he's *still* performing at the highest level. He's even had the opportunity to play alongside his eldest child, Bronny, in the LA Lakers!

LeBron James (left) and Bronny James (right)

The future

All over the world, basketball is growing, and the future of the sport looks incredible.

In the US, the NBA continues to attract players from across the globe, who are thirsty for victory! French player, Victor Wembanyama, is one to watch. He's a staggering 224 cm and has a vertical reach of 386 cm!

The WNBA is turning players like Angel Reese and Caitlin Clark into superstars.

Victor Wembanyama

Caitlin Clark (left) and Angel Reese (right)

In the UK, basketball is being played in more schools and hoops are appearing in more parks. The sport continues to grow.

Winning matters. But basketball's life lessons in persistence, work ethic, team spirit, diversity and inclusivity matter even more.

A look at streetball

Streetball is a less formal take on basketball. The focus is on playfulness, skill, style and flair. Tricks and attitude are as important as winning, and streetball needs nothing more than a ball!

Rucker Park in New York, US, is seen as the home of streetball.

How do streetball and basketball differ?

- Streetball is played outside in informal settings, typically in parks and on streets.
- Streetball is more relaxed and every game has its own rules. Often, there's no referee. Instead, players keep count of the score and look out for fouls themselves.
- The points are different. For example, a throw that's worth three points in basketball might get two points in streetball.
- Most streetball games have three players on each team, but you can play one against one. A basketball game has five players per side.
- Streetball often starts with a 'pick-up game'. Anyone can say they want to play, and two players called 'captains' take turns picking players for their team.

Ouch!

Written by Tom Watt

Illustrated by Filippo Pietrobon

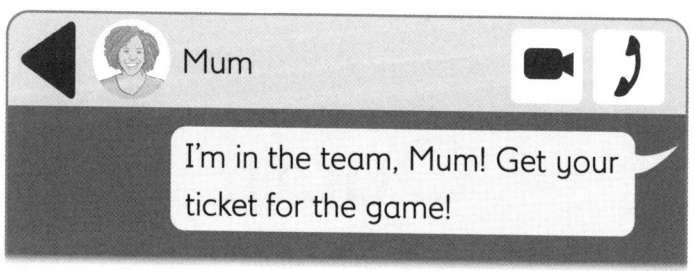

Mum

I'm in the team, Mum! Get your ticket for the game!

It had all been going so well. At just 18, Steve Prince had burst into Portland Town's first team. The fans worshipped him. The boss trusted him, and so did the other players. Steve had just scored his third goal in nine games. People were even saying the England manager had an eye on him!

It was nearly full-time, and Steve was hurtling down the pitch with the ball at his feet. Next thing he knew, he was on the ground, curled up in agony. It felt as if a lightning bolt had struck the back of his leg. It was the worst pain imaginable. Everything was a blur.

The club doctor ran onto the pitch and asked, "Where does it hurt, Steve?"

Portland Town Times

YOUNG TOWN STAR'S INJURY CONFIRMED

The next day, Steve woke up in hospital, fearing the worst. The club doctor walked in. She told Steve that his leg surgery had gone well.

"How long before I can play again?" Steve asked.

"As long as it takes. You'll need to rest up and heal," the doctor replied.

"And that's an order!" she added, firmly.

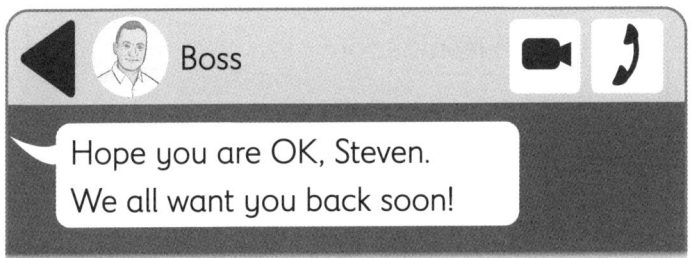

For two weeks, Steve was stuck at home. He watched sport on TV, gamed or just gazed out the window. Time crawled by. Steve was so bored! He wasn't used to sitting around – he needed to be playing. Football was his whole world, after all.

Finally, he got an email from the club doctor.

> To: SteveP14@mail.com
>
> Subject: Gym @ 2:00 p.m.
>
> Hi Steve,
>
> Please report to the club gym at 2:00 p.m. Time to start working on your fitness!
>
> Regards,
>
> Doc

At first, it was great to be back. Steve worked as hard as he could in the gym. But it was lonely and, worst of all, he'd arrive at the training ground each day just as the other players were leaving.

Every time he felt pain anywhere, Steve couldn't help thinking, *Is my time on the pitch over for good?*

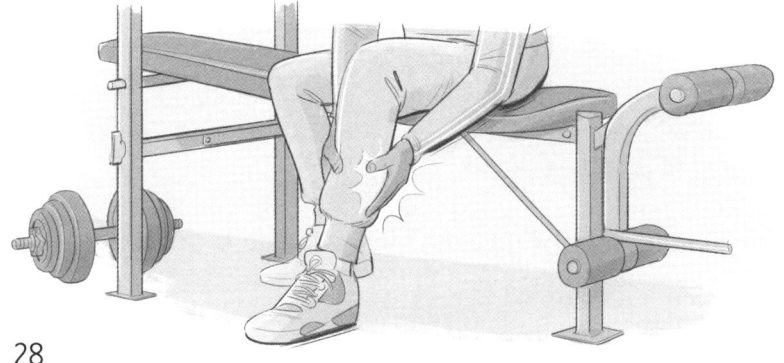

The message from his friend Jimmy really boosted Steve's spirits. The following evening, he went out with all the other players. They laughed and joked together and, for the first time in ages, Steve felt he was still part of the team.

When he went into the gym the next day, his mood had shifted. It felt as if he had something to aim for now.

It was a real boost for Steve to know that the boss was thinking about him. It stirred up a lot of feelings. It made the long, lonely haul to recovery feel worthwhile. In fact, it made Steve even more determined to come back stronger.

So, he worked harder than ever. He came home each evening, sore and exhausted. Mum would put dinner in front of him, he'd watch a match on TV and then fall into bed.

Steve could sense he was almost 100% fit again.

To: SteveP14@mail.com

Subject: Training @ 10:00 a.m.

Hi Steve,

Pleased to confirm you are ready to return to full training. Report at 10:00 a.m. tomorrow morning.

Regards,

Doc

Steve arrived at the training ground before everyone else – he couldn't wait to join in again. His team-mates were pleased to see him, too. First, they did some stretches together. Next, they went through practice drills. Almost straightaway, Steve felt like he was back where he belonged, out on the pitch with a ball at his feet.

At the end of the morning, the boss set up a 7-a-side match and asked Steve to join in. He ran as fast as ever and even scored a couple of goals.

Then, just before the end of the game, his team-mate slid in and tackled him. Steve felt a burst of pain in his leg.

Ouch! That hurt!

He lay on the cold ground, blinking at the sky, unable to talk. The rest of the players gathered round.

Steve took a deep breath. He looked up and saw all the worried faces. The other lads were fearing the worst. Steve was worried, too.

But after a few seconds, he realised his leg wasn't hurting any more. In that moment, Steve knew he was going to be OK.

"I'm fine," he said with relief. He grinned at his friends, wiping dirt off his leg.

Steve hauled himself to his feet, knowing his leg had passed its first big test. Being able to take a tough tackle like that confirmed to everyone that he was ready to play again.

Steve had returned to full training. But being on the fringe of the first team for so long made him worried. They had been doing well without him. Would he be worthy of a spot in the starting line-up? He promised himself that he'd give it everything.

In the days that followed, Steve ran faster than anyone else. He worked harder in the gym. He scored goals in every practice game. Would the boss notice?

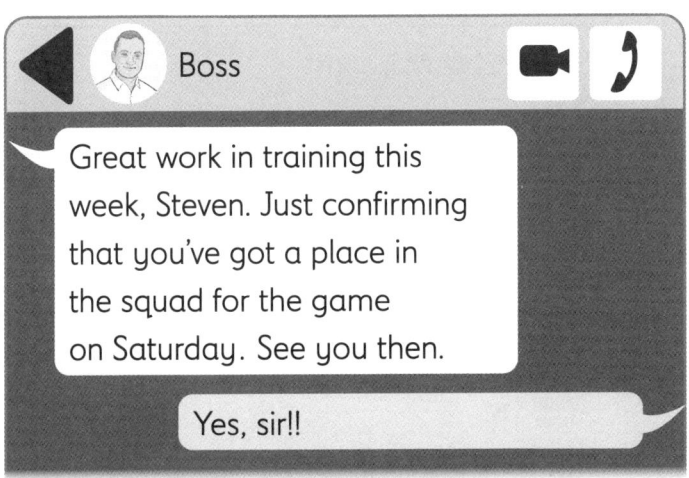

Boss

Great work in training this week, Steven. Just confirming that you've got a place in the squad for the game on Saturday. See you then.

Yes, sir!!

When he saw the message saying he was in the matchday squad, Steve punched the air. It felt like scoring a goal. His hard work had been worth it!

He was excited at first, but then the nerves kicked in. Would he cope with the pace of a real match? Would his leg survive a real tackle? Would he even get on the pitch to find out? He was only on the bench, after all.

To: SteveP14@mail.com

Subject: Steve's back!

The final hurdle. Good luck!

Doc

Good luck, Stevie! Proud being your mum!! xxx

Steve's big moment arrived after 75 minutes. The score was 0–0. The boss called him over, wanting to talk.

"Go out and grab a goal!" he told Steve. "There's still time to win us the game!"

There's only one Stevie Prince!

The crowd was calling Steve's name, willing him to get on the scoresheet. He took off his tracksuit and put on his shin pads. He felt his heart pounding under his shirt, so he took a long, deep breath.

Steve knew he'd put in the work after his injury. He knew he'd pushed through every obstacle and cleared every hurdle.

Now was his chance to show those Portland Town fans that Steve Prince was back!

Pathway to pro football

How do football players develop into pro stars? Every route and timeline differs. Some clubs recommend a pathway like this:

Garden or park (age 4–6)
Playing for fun sparks enjoyment of football.

Youth academy (age 11–15)
Players train multiple times a week. They are coached by qualified coaches and sports scientists.

Under 21s
The last step. Some players are promoted to the first team. Some transfer to other clubs' senior squads.

Less than 1% of teenage academy players reach the top levels of pro football!

School and local teams (age 6–8)
Players develop a basic understanding of the rules, team play and skills.

Club camps (age 7–11)
These are a bridge between local teams and formal football. Young talent is often spotted at this point.

Under 18s
The first step into pro football. This involves two years of full-time training and school tutoring.

First team
The final goal! Players train and compete full time with the club's senior squad.

Going for Gold

Written by Tom Watt

The greatest show on Earth

Every four years, people around the world come together for the 'greatest show on Earth': the Olympic Games. We watch athletes create amazing moments in sporting history.

Rome, 1960: Bikila, from Ethiopia, became the first African Olympic gold medallist when he won the marathon. He ran barefoot.

From the arrival of the Olympic torch at the opening ceremony, to the exciting atmosphere at each event, the Olympics is a time to celebrate what people from all over the world can achieve.

Beijing (say: *bai-jing*), 2008: Bolt, known as 'the fastest man on Earth', won gold for Jamaica in both the 100 and 200 metres.

How did the Olympic Games begin?

The Olympic Games began in Greece in 776 BCE, over 2,800 years ago. Only men took part … and they didn't wear any clothes! These naked athletes competed for up to six months to show respect for the Olympic gods.

Relics at the site of the original Olympic Games in Greece.

The first 13 Olympic Games only included one running race. Over time, more events were added, like long jump, wrestling, boxing and chariot racing.

A marble slab showing a chariot.

As far as we're aware, 291 Olympic Games were held in Greece until a Roman ruler banned them. Women didn't compete at all until 1900! To hear more about that, let's explore the modern Olympics.

Who started the modern Olympic Games?

Over 1,500 years after the Olympic Games were banned, a teacher from France decided to bring them back. He cared about sport because he said it was an important way to educate people. He wanted to make sport more popular worldwide, so he set up an Olympic Committee in 1894 to restart the Games.

The founder of the modern Olympic Games, Baron de Coubertin (say: *coo-bair-tan*).

The first modern Olympic Games were held in 1896 in Athens, Greece. Just 245 male competitors from 11 countries competed. Compared to now, that's not very many athletes. However, at the time, the Games were the biggest global sporting event ever.

Athens, 1896: Local hero, Louis (say: *loo-ee*), won gold for Greece in the marathon.

In 2024, 206 countries sent over 10,000 athletes to compete in the Paris Games.

What about women?

Only men were allowed to compete in the first modern Olympic Games. However, one woman dared to run the marathon the day after the men's race. Stamata Revithi ran barefoot with her wooden slippers in her hands and finished the race on her own. She declared, "If the committee doesn't let me compete, I will go after them regardless!"

Athens, 1896: A Greek woman, Revithi, ran the marathon before women were allowed to compete in the Olympics.

Revithi's words may have helped change people's minds. Four years later, women competed in some events at the 1900 Paris Games, but they made up a mere two percent of the athletes. Today, male and female athletes compete in equal numbers and in every sport.

Paris, 1900: An English tennis player, Cooper, was the first woman to win an individual gold medal at the Olympics.

When could sledders and skaters compete?

The modern Olympic Games were popular from the start. Winter sports athletes, who competed on snow and ice, wanted to experience the atmosphere, too. However, they had to wait until 1924 for the first Winter Olympics in France.

The Winter Olympics have been part of the global sporting calendar ever since. They are smaller than the summer event but just as thrilling!

Beijing, 2022: The men's final of the short-track speed skating.

Chamonix (say: *sham-o-nee*), 1924: Figure skater, Henie, was only 11 when she competed for Norway in the first Winter Olympics. She finished last but persevered and won gold medals at the next three Winter Olympics.

When did the Paralympics begin?

Cities around the world compete to host the Olympic Games, and in 1960 it was Rome's turn. The 1960 Rome Games were important for a few reasons. All the events were shown on TV for the first time, which allowed a huge worldwide audience to share in the excitement. It was also here that the Paralympics began!

Beijing, 2008: Cities prepare for years to host the Olympic and Paralympic Games. Organisers in Beijing took great care to make venues accessible. They also built lifts and wheelchair ramps at popular places around China, including the Great Wall of China.

The Paralympics are now the second biggest sporting event in the world. Millions of people watch over 4,500 athletes with disabilities compete every four years.

Paris, 2024: Swiss wheelchair racer, Debrunner, won five gold medals. She led the marathon from start to finish.

What's the story behind the Olympic torch?

The Olympic torch appears at every opening ceremony to mark the start of the Games. The idea for the torch came from the first Olympics in Greece, where a flame was kept burning in the Temple of Hera. The flame returned to the modern Olympics in 1928. In 1936, it was lit in Greece, and travelled over 3,187 km to Berlin, carried by 3,331 runners in 12 days!

Atlanta, 1996: Despite having a serious illness, gold-medallist boxer Muhammad Ali walked slowly into the arena bearing the torch to start the Atlanta Games. Many people consider this one of the most powerful moments in Olympic history.

Since 1936, the torch has always started in Greece and travelled across countries and continents to reach the opening ceremony. It represents the spirit of the Olympics and the shared bond between people and countries during the Games.

Sydney, 2000: A diver carried an underwater flare across the Great Barrier Reef on the way to the 2000 Sydney Games. The torch has even been into space!

Gold medal records

It's a fantastic achievement to win a gold medal at the Olympics or Paralympics. But look at these Olympic and Paralympic heroes who have won more than one!

Summer Olympics

Name: Phelps
Country: US
Sport: Swimming
Number of gold medals: 23

Name: Latynina
Country: USSR
Sport: Gymnastics
Number of gold medals: 9

Phelps got a record for the most medals at a single Olympics. In the 2008 Beijing Games, he won 8 golds – one for each event he entered.

Winter Olympics

Name: Bjørgen
(say: *b-yor-gen*)
Country: Norway
Sport: Skiing
Number of gold medals: 8

Name: Bjørndalen
(say: *b-yorn-dalen*)
Country: Norway
Sport: Biathlon
Number of gold medals: 8

Paralympics

Name: Zorn
Country: US
Sport: Swimming
Number of gold medals: 41

Name: Jacobsson
Country: Sweden
Sport: Shooting
Number of gold medals: 17

From Zero To Hero

Written by Chris Bradford

Illustrated by Douglas Lopes

I stare hard at my opponent, Viper. She walks around the ring, trying to scare me. I pretend not to care but my heart is pounding.

The bell rings and applause erupts from the crowd. The atmosphere in the arena is electric. It's the first year wushu has been part of the Youth Olympic Games.

But what if my fears are true? What if I'm not good enough to represent my country?

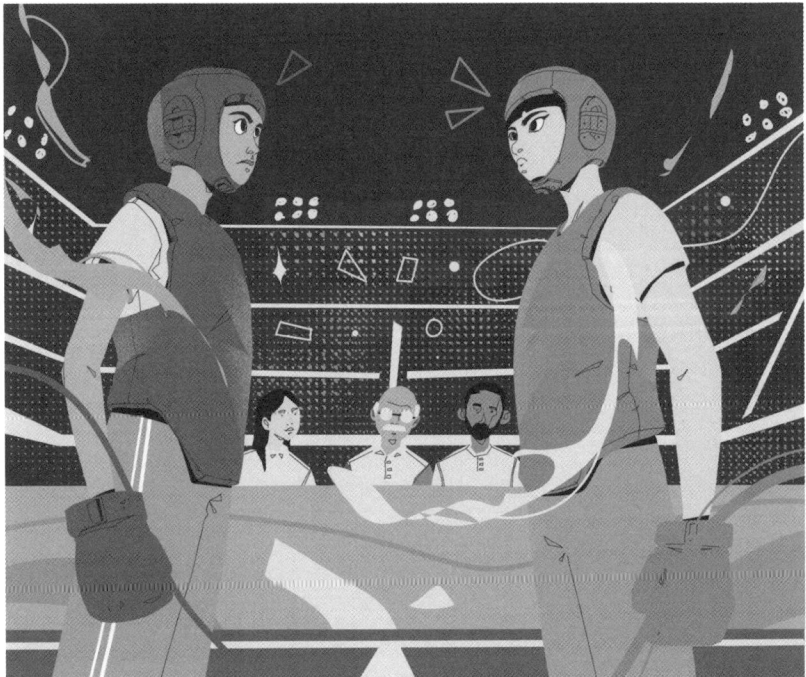

Viper hurtles over to me. She throws a jab, then a rear cross, followed by an upper cut. The vast number of punches overwhelms me. She catches my ear with a back fist.

"Point, Viper!" announces the ref.

Before I can recover, she tears into me again. A front kick sends me hurtling into the ropes.

"Point, Viper!"

As I gasp for breath, she flips me over her shoulder. I crash onto the mat.

"Point, Viper! Three-zero," declares the ref. "Winner, Viper!"

The match is over. In mere seconds, I've lost.

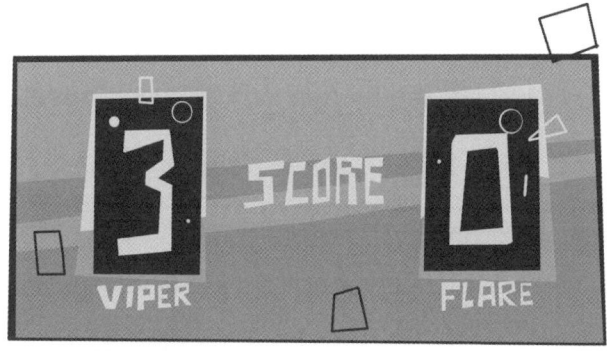

As I stagger to my corner, I hear the crowd shout, "Zero! Zero!"

My coach, Sifu Cheng, pulls up a chair for me.

"I'm so bad," I mutter.

"Chin up, Flare," he replies, gently. "You learn more from defeat than victory."

I stare at the ground, my eyes blurring with tears. "I've learned I'm the world's worst wushu athlete!"

"There's always next year," he consoles me.

The crowd erupts as another match begins. But I just want to disappear, so I collect my gear and head to the exit.

Outside, we wait by the kerb for our taxi.

As the car pulls up, I swear I hear my name. I turn to see a woman in a suit running over to me.

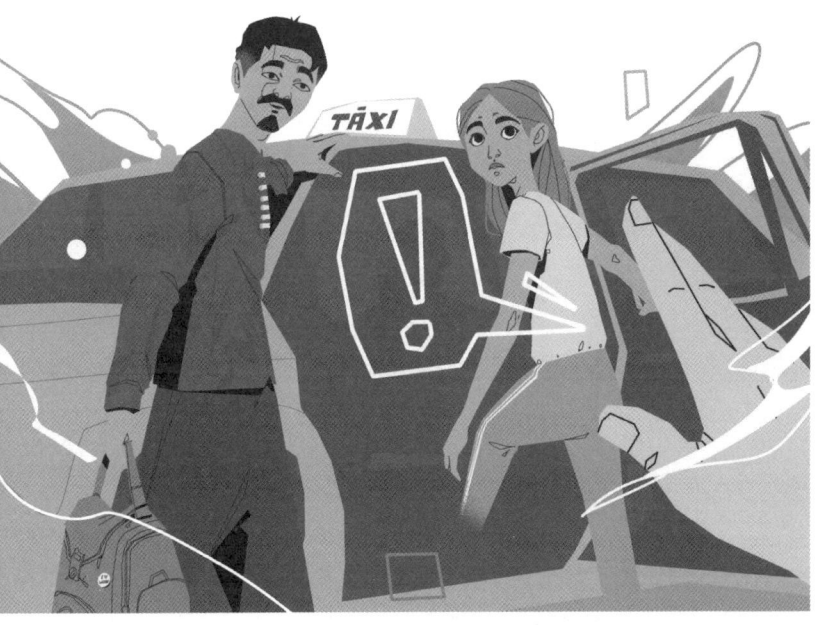

"Flare, you need to stay here!" she says. "You are a lucky loser!"

I frown. "What does that mean?"

"A competitor has dropped out," the woman explains. "You get another chance!"

We return to the arena, where my opponent is waiting for me in the ring. She's the size of a bear!

"This isn't fair!" I say.

Sifu shrugs. "The bigger they are, the harder they fall."

I stare at Sifu. "Yes, fall on top of *me*!"

As I climb into the ring, the crowd chants, "Zero! Zero!"

Compared to Bear, I'm puny. She's much taller and her arms are pure muscle. Her upper lip curls into a snarl as she looks down at me.

The bell rings. Round one. I stare like a rabbit in headlights, frozen to the spot. Bear grounds me with one strike.

"Point, Bear!" the ref declares.

I stagger over to Sifu. "She's going to tear me up!"

"Bear is slow," he tells me. "Move like the wind."

I nod, sort of understanding.

Round two. Bear hurls her massive fist, but I dodge to one side. She comes at me again. This time, I twist and turn like the wind. She can't get near me.

I begin to wear her down. Her punches and kicks get slower but I need some spare energy, too. The crowd yells, frustrated by our performance.

Bear clips my chin.

"Zero! Zero!" the crowd chants. I stumble. Another point to Bear.

I turn to Sifu. "This isn't working!"

"Chop the tree down!" he replies.

I've no clue what he means.

Round three. I'm running, scared, avoiding Bear's brutal blows. She squares up and delivers a roundhouse kick. Her left leg is rooted, as stable as a tree.

Of course! Chop the tree!

I drop low, spin round and sweep out her leg. Bear crashes to the mat, falling like a tree.

"Point, Flare!" the ref shouts. "And knockout!" he adds in disbelief.

There's a murmur of astonishment from the crowd. My opponent is so winded by her fall, she can't get back up.

I tear over to Sifu Cheng. "It worked!"

Sifu grins. "I told you: the bigger they are, the harder they fall."

I've won my first fight!

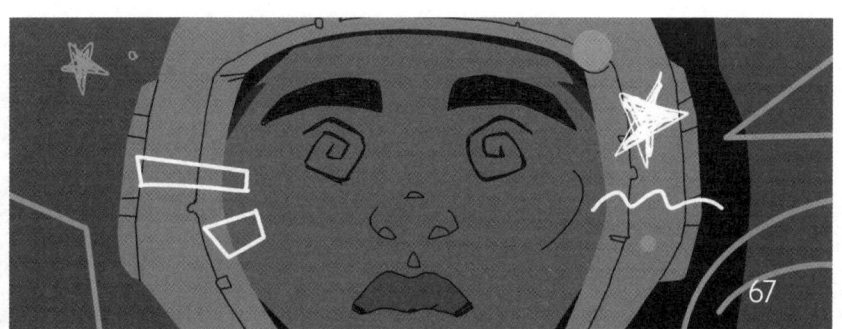

But we don't get long to celebrate.
My next match is against River,
an athlete as tall and slender as a reed.

The bell rings. River glides across
the mat like she's floating on water.
Her limbs ebb and flow like waves,
making her attacks hard to block.
She wins the first point, then the second
just as easily.

Sifu beckons me over and says, "A river flows, but fire erupts."

I stare at him. *Why does he always have to talk in riddles?*

"Break her flow," he adds.

Back on the mat, I unleash explosive bursts with no pattern. This disrupts River's flow, and I score a point. Then another. I aim a front kick that hits her square in the chest. That's the third point.

I win!

For my third match, I face Terra, a shorter, heavily muscled athlete. She wears an earth-brown *gi*.

"Terra prefers groundwork," says Sifu. "So don't get too close."

But that's easier said than done. Terra ensnares my arm, holding it in a trap, and hurls me into the air.

"Point, Terra!"

Chants of "Zero! Zero!" thunder through the arena again.

"Take to the air!" Sifu calls.

Terra charges at me. I jump over her, launching a back kick.

"Point, Flare!"

Every time Terra comes close, I leap into the air. Two quick points later and I'm the winner! The arena fills with joy.

I can't believe it! I'm in the final!

"One last hurdle," Sifu says as Viper slinks back into the ring.

Terror grips me. "I've no chance against *her*!"

Sifu clasps my shoulder. "Remember, you learn more from defeat than victory."

I glare at him. *Now is not the time for more riddles.*

"Speed is her weapon," he tells me. "But you are Flare – blind the snake with your light."

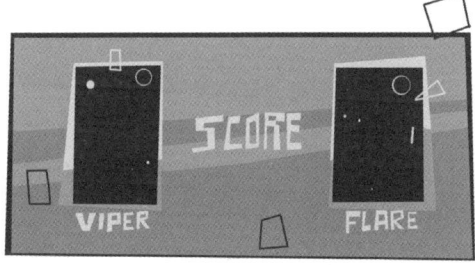

I step back into the ring for the fifth and final time.

"Prepare for your worst nightmare, Zero!" Viper smirks.

The bell rings. Viper attacks with a blur of punches. Two points are gone in seconds – just like the first match. Someone in the crowd chants, "Zero! Zero!"

I'm close to defeat. What can I do?

Blind the snake with your light ...

I shift closer to the press pit. The bright glare of the cameras dazzles Viper. I land a punch, winning me a vital point. Viper attacks again but this time I twist like a flame. I shift left, then strike right.

Two all.

Angry, Viper lunges and drives her elbow into my back. I crumple.

"Foul!" yells the ref.

I'm scared – my back hurts.

I make it back to my corner. "I can't go on," I groan, as the crowd chants, "Zero! Zero!"

"You must," insists Sifu. "They're chanting ... for *you*."

I finally hear the real words from the crowd: "Hero! Hero!"

I rise back to my feet. The bell rings. As Viper prepares to strike, I rear up and let loose a spinning kick. It lands square on her jaw.

"Match point!"

Sifu jumps into the ring and lifts me into the air. "From zero ... to HERO!"

The rules of wushu

Wushu is also called kung fu. It was first added to the Youth Olympic Games in 2026. There are two main sorts of wushu. Flare competes in *Sanda*, which is full-contact combat wushu.

Allowed moves
- Punches to the head or body
- Kicks to the legs, body or head
- Safe throws and takedowns

Disallowed moves
- No hits to the back of the head, throat or spine
- No elbows, headbutts, joint locks or choking
- No dangerous slams

Scoring
- High points: throws, knockdowns and head kicks
- Medium: strong body kicks and controlled throws
- Low: clean punches and light kicks

How to win
- Score more points than your opponent
- Your opponent gets fouls
- Your opponent cannot continue

Qualities of an Olympic pro
- Strong control
- Good balance
- Accurate skill
- Bold spirit

Acknowledgements

The publishers gratefully acknowledge the permission granted to reproduce the copyright material in this book. Every effort has been made to trace copyright holders and to obtain their permission for the use of copyright material. The publishers will gladly receive any information enabling them to rectify any error or omission at the first opportunity.

p6 Mark Ralston/Getty Images, p7 matimix/Shutterstock, p8 Fernando Medina/NBAE/Getty Images, p9 Robert Abbott Sengstacke/Getty Images, p10 Andrew D. Bernstein/NBAE/Getty Images, p11 Jessica Hill/Associated Press/Alamy Stock Photo, p12 Nigel French via PAMA/PA Images/Alamy Stock Photo, p13 samuel perales/Shutterstock, p14 Matthew Stockman/Getty Images, p15l Tina Fultz/ZUMA Press/Alamy Stock Photo, p15r John W. McDonough/Associated Press/Alamy Stock Photo, p16 Ron Waite/Cal Sport Media/Alamy Stock Photo, p17t UPI Photo/Scott R. Galvin/Alamy Stock Photo, p17b Mitchell Leff/Getty Images, p18l Laurent Zabulon/ABACAPRESS.COM/Alamy Stock Photo, p18r Andy Lyons/Getty Images, p19 Ryan Pierse/Getty Images, pp20–21 Ishika Samant/Getty Images, p42 The History Collection/Alamy Stock Photo, p43 photoyh/Shutterstock, p44 Todamo/Shutterstock, p+B2645 byruineves/Shutterstock, p46 Cci/Shutterstock, p47t Hi-Story/Alamy Stock Photo, p47b Vitalii Vitleo/Shutterstock, p48 Wikimedia Commons, p49 Chronicle/Alamy Stock Photo, p50 Mickael Chavet /RX/Alamy Stock Photo, p51 Popperfoto/Getty Images, p52 ABCDstock/Shutterstock, p53 Thibault Camus/Associated Press/Alamy Stock Photo, p54 Associated Press/Alamy Stock Photo, p55 Steve Nutt/ALLSPORT/Getty Images, p56l Focus Pix/Shutterstock, p56r Smith Archive/Alamy Stock Photo, p57tl Lise Aaserud/NTB/Alamy Stock Photo, p57tr Jon Eeg/NTB/Alamy Stock Photo, p57bl Sean Garnsworthy/ALLSPORT/Getty Images, p57br Elizabeth Dalziel/Associated Press/Alamy Stock Photo, p74t CHEN WS/Shutterstock, pp74–75 CHEN WS/Shutterstock.

Published by Collins
An imprint of HarperCollins*Publishers*
The News Building, 1 London Bridge Street, London, SE1 9GF, UK

HarperCollins*Publishers*
Macken House, 39/40 Mayor Street Upper, Dublin 1, D01 C9W8, Ireland

Browse the complete Collins catalogue at
collins.co.uk

'From Zero To Hero' text © Chris Bradford 2026
All other text, illustrations and design © HarperCollins*Publishers* Limited 2026

Wandle Learning Trust name and logo © Wandle Learning Trust

10 9 8 7 6 5 4 3 2 1

A catalogue record for this publication is available from the British Library.

ISBN 978-0-00-879100-1

All rights reserved. No part of this publication may be reproduced, stored in a retrieval system, or transmitted in any form by any means, electronic, mechanical, photocopying, recording or otherwise, without the prior written permission of the Publisher or a licence permitting restricted copying in the United Kingdom issued by the Copyright Licensing Agency Ltd, 5th Floor, Shackleton House, 4 Battle Bridge Lane, London SE1 2HX.

Without limiting the exclusive rights of any author, contributor or the publisher of this publication, any unauthorised use of this publication to train generative artificial intelligence (AI) technologies is expressly prohibited. HarperCollins also exercise their rights under Article 4(3) of the Digital Single Market Directive 2019/790 and expressly reserve this publication from the text and data mining exception.

Authors: Chris Bradford, Jonny Walker and Tom Watt
Illustrators: Filippo Pietrobon (Beehive Illustration) and Douglas Lopes (Illo Agency)
Publisher: Katie Sergeant
Product manager: Natasha Paul
Education consultant: Charlotte Raby
Project manager: Emily Hooton
Phonics reviewers: Catherine Baker and Abbie Rushton
Proofreader and fact checker: Catherine Dakin
Cover designer: Sarah Finan
Cover image: Brian Jackson/Alamy
Internal designer: 2Hoots Publishing Services Ltd
Production controller: Sophie Waeland

Developed in collaboration with Wandle Learning Trust

Printed in the UK by Martins the Printers

MIX
Paper | Supporting responsible forestry
FSC www.fsc.org FSC™ C013254

Made with responsibly sourced paper and vegetable ink

Scan to see how we are reducing our environmental impact.

Collins would like to thank Abi Rothe, Nicola Dickens and the schools involved in the Code pilot for contributing to the development of this book.

Access the planning and resources to teach this book at littlewandlecode.org.uk